THE ELSON READERS—BOOK ONE
A Teacher's Guide

Cynthia Keel Landen
M.A., Educational Leadership; B.A., Early Childhood and Elementary Education; Elementary Teacher/Babson Park Elementary School

Lorrie Driggers Phillips
M.A., Curriculum and Instruction; B.A., Early Childhood and Elementary Education; Elementary Teacher/Babson Park Elementary School

Lost Classics Book Company
Lake Wales, Florida

PUBLISHER'S NOTE

Recognizing the need to return to more traditional principles in education, Lost Classics Book Company is republishing forgotten late 19th and early 20th century literature and textbooks to aid parents in the education of their children.

The Elson Readers—Book One, which this volume is meant to accompany, has been assigned a reading level of 270L. More information concerning this reading level assessment may be attained by visiting www.lexile.com.

The Authors

Cynthia Keel Landen graduated with degrees in early childhood and elementary education from the University of Florida. She earned her master's degree in educational leadership at the University of South Florida. She is an elementary teacher with eighteen years of experience and is currently teaching fifth grade at Babson Park Elementary School in Babson Park, Florida.

Lorrie Driggers Phillips graduated from Florida Southern College with degrees in early childhood and elementary education. She received her master's degree in curriculum and instruction from the University of Southern Mississippi. She taught for thirteen years.

© Copyright 2005
Lost Classics Book Company
ISBN 978-1-890623-25-8
Designed to Accompany
The Elson Readers—Book One
ISBN 978-1-890623-15-9
Part of
The Elson Readers
Nine Volumes: *Primer* through *Book Eight*
ISBN 978-1-890623-23-4

On the Cover:
The Tortoise and the Hare from Aesop's Fables, pub. by Raphael Tuck & Sons Ltd., London (book illustration) by John Edwin Noble
Private Collection/Bridgeman Art Library
Lost Classics Book Company would also like to thank Lewis Noble, grandson of John Edwin Noble, for his kind assistance.

TABLE OF CONTENTS

THE ELSON READERS—BOOK ONE
A TEACHER'S GUIDE

HOW TO USE THIS BOOK

The *Elson Readers, Book One* is filled with delightful stories and fables for your child to learn from and enjoy. Many life lessons are taught in the fables through the adventures of the adorable characters.

The following suggestions help your child to have continued successes in reading and writing at this level: Keep a vocabulary journal in a notebook, provide daily opportunities for drawing and writing, and read to your child, or have the child read independently daily. Keep in mind that if your child is not reading independently yet, your model of reading will promote this skill.

Lists of words will be provided for each story. We suggest that your child learn these words prior to reading the stories. One way of teaching the words is for you or your child to write one word at the top of a page in the vocabulary journal. Your child can then draw a picture that illustrates the word. As your child becomes more literate, he or she can use the new word in a sentence on the same page. Another method for learning and reviewing the vocabulary words is by using index cards. The words can go on one side of the card and the pictures on the other. These cards are great for reviewing all the words.

It is important to keep in mind that reading is more than just calling words on the page. True reading is when you read something and can understand what the author is trying to convey. You will find comprehension questions for most of the stories and fables in this book. The questions will be written in one of four formats. The formats include: *literal, implied, vocabulary,* and *creative.*

Literal questions are answered right in the story. An example of a literal question is: What is the little boy's pet? *Implied* questions are not literally written in the text. Clues and background knowledge are used to answer questions such as: What time of year is it in this story? Children will look at the pictures and see, for example, children wearing jackets and building a snowman. They can infer that it is winter because building a snowman is a winter activity. Have your child give a reason for his or her implied questions either in oral or written form. You can use the answers provided as a model of how your child could respond. *Vocabulary* questions review or explore deeper meanings from the words in the story. *Creative* questions are where children can dream and be unique. This provides a great opportunity for children to tell, draw, or write about their creations. With the fables, children may be asked to tell the lesson of the story.

There will be more literal and implied questions included than vocabulary and creative questions. Literal and implied questions indicate story comprehension more directly than vocabulary and creative questions. At this stage of development, students should be moving into writing their answers on paper. Depending on your child's written skills, it may be more successful to only answer questions orally at first. By doing the questions orally, the child is free to concentrate on his or her answer instead of laboring over the mechanics of writing. When you feel the time is right, ease into the idea of writing the answers down. Start with only a few questions and work up to the entire comprehension lesson. Whether your child is answering the questions orally or written, have the child give the answers in complete sentences by stating part of the question in the answer. See the answers to the comprehension questions for examples.

Most stories will be provided with skills and phonics lessons. Skills are defined on the worksheets and answers are provided. Phonics will be basic lessons on long and short vowel sounds and blends with beginning and ending sounds. A hint with long vowels is that the letter says its name. For example, the word *closed* says the letter *o* sound when spoken. Short vowels can be more complicated. The lessons will concentrate on the regular short vowel sounds. There are other vowel sounds that are controlled by an *r*. When you see an *r* next to a vowel, it changes the way the vowel sounds. For example, the word *car* does not have a short or long vowel sound. The *a* is *r* controlled. We did not include lessons in here with *r* controlled vowels because long and short vowels need to be mastered first. We have given you the vowel sounds or blends to focus on for each selection.

There are many approaches to practicing the sounds. You can have your child cut pictures or words from newspapers and magazines to match the sounds, your child can brainstorm other words to go with the set, or you can search the story or a story you've read for words with particular sounds. Another idea is for you to provide pictures or word cards to classify into sounds. A great way to practice the long vowel sounds is by having the letters of the alphabet on small pieces of paper and fitting them into the template __a__e, to create words with the vowel sounds you are working on.

Always have lined and unlined paper and many writing tools on hand for your child. Children need to have their fine motor skills exercised by having many opportunities to draw and write. A great way to work on writing is to have your child draw a picture. You can then dictate what the child wants to say about the picture.

A Note about This Guide

Teachers and students alike may notice a difference in punctuation, capitalization, and spelling between the prose and poetry sections in the reader. Rules for these matters have changed since the original reader's publication, and we have decided that in the prose sections it would be in the best interest of the student to update these items so they will learn these rules as practiced today. However, the stories remain completely unabridged. We have exercised constraint, and typical changes consist of, for example: commas used in place of semicolons when appropriate, lowercase treatment of words not personified, or hyphenated spelling of words being contracted to modern spellings. We have, however, followed the traditional editorial practice of not changing these items in works of poetry, leaving these matters to the prerogative of the poet.

We have used *The Chicago Manual of Style,* 14th Edition, published by the University of Chicago, as our primary reference for these changes.

Objectives—

By completing *Book One,* the following objectives will be met:

1. The student will predict what a story is about based on its title and illustrations.
2. The student will identify words and construct meaning from text, illustrations, use of phonics, and context clues.
3. The student will use knowledge of developmental-level vocabulary in reading.
4. The student will increase comprehension by retelling and discussion.
5. The student will determine the main idea and supporting details from text.
6. The student will select material to read for pleasure.
7. The student will know strategies to use to discover whether information presented in a text is true, including asking others and checking another source.
8. The student will use simple reference materials to obtain information.
9. The student will make a plan for writing that includes a central idea and related ideas.
10. The student will show an awareness of a beginning, middle, and end in passages.
11. The student will produce final simple documents that have been edited for: correct spelling, appropriate end punctuation, correct capitalization of initial words, correct sentence structure, and correct usage of age appropriate subject/verb and noun/ pronoun agreement.
12. The student will write questions and observations about familiar topics, stories, or new experiences.
13. The student will use knowledge and experience to tell about experiences or to write for familiar occasions, audiences, and purposes.
14. The student will follow simple sets of instructions for simple tasks using logical sequencing of steps.
15. The student will listen for a variety of purposes, including curiosity, pleasure, getting directions, performing tasks, solving problems, and following rules.
16. The student will retell details of information heard, including sequence of events.
17. The student will determine the main idea through illustrations.
18. The student will speak clearly and at a volume audible in large or small group settings.
19. The student will recognize basic patterns in and functions of language.
20. The student will understand that word choice can shape ideas, feelings, and actions.
21. The student will identify and use repetition, rhyme, and rhythm in oral and written text.
22. The student will recognize that use of more than one medium increases the power to influence how one thinks and feels.
23. The student will know the basic characteristics of fables, stories, and legends.
24. The student will identify the story elements of setting, plot, character, problem, and solution.
25. The student will use personal perspective in responding to a work of literature, such as relating characters and simple events in a story or biography to people or events in his or her own life.
26. The student will recognize rhymes, rhythm, and patterned structures in children's texts.

LITTLE GUSTAVA, P. 9

Preteach and review the following vocabulary: spring, sun, bread, wings, winter, gray, brown, and white.

After reading the story with your child a couple times, answer the following comprehension questions.

Literal

1. Why was Gustava so happy? Gustava was happy because spring had come and she loved spring.

Implied

2. How did Gustava know it was spring? Gustava knew spring had come because she heard a bird singing and felt the warm sun.

Literal

3. What animals came to see Gustava? Gustava was visited by Little Gray Kitten, Brown Hen, the White Doves, and Little Dog.

Implied

4. Why was it easier for the White Doves to find food in spring than in winter? During winter there is usually snow on the ground and plants and bushes are usually bare.

Literal

5. How much milk did Gustava tell Little Dog he could have? Gustava told Little Dog to take all the milk he wanted.

Implied

6. Why did Gustava have no dinner? Gustava had no dinner because she gave her food to the animals.

Creative

7. What do you think Gustava will do with the new bread and milk that her mother gives her? Gustava will probably eat the bread and milk because the animals had eaten but Gustava had not.

The phonics lesson is the long *a* sound found in the word *name*. Other words from the story are *gave, came, gray,* and *away.* Long *a* words can have a final *e* and can be spelled with *ay*.

An extension to this story would be to draw or paint pictures of activities enjoyed in the four seasons.

Answers:

1. bow-wow 2. mew-mew 3. cluck-cluck

1. clock 2. mouse, toy 3. duck, fish 4. car, truck (Accept other reasonable answers.)

LITTLE GUSTAVA, p. 9

An onomatopoeia is a word that makes the sound the word stands for. Examples of this type of word are: buzz, hiss, coo-coo. See if you can find three more onomatopoeia words from the story and list them here.

1. _____

2. _____

3. _____

Then draw pictures to match the given onomatopoeia words:

1. tick-tock

2. squeak-squeak

3. splish-splash

4. varoom-varoom

WHO TOOK THE BIRD'S NEST?, P. 15

Preteach and review the following vocabulary: brook, nest, hairs, wool, yellow, black, and beautiful.

Answer the following comprehension questions.

Literal

1. What is Yellow Bird's problem? Yellow Bird cannot find the nest she built.

Implied

2. What did Yellow Bird use to build her nest? Yellow Bird used hay, hair, and wool. (Accept other reasonable additions to the answer, for example twigs, moss, etc.)

Literal

3. Who did Yellow Bird ask if they took her nest? Yellow Bird asked White Cow, Brown Dog, and Black Sheep if they had taken her nest.

Literal

4. Who took Yellow Bird's nest? The little boy took Yellow Bird's nest.

Implied

5. Why did the little boy hang his head, hide behind the bed, and not eat his dinner? The little boy hung his head, hid, and would not eat because he felt guilty for taking Yellow Bird's nest.

Vocabulary

6. Name three things you might find in a *brook*. You might find fish, frogs, or rocks in a brook. (Accept any reasonable answers.)

Creative

7. What do you think the little boy did after he gave the nest back? (Accept any reasonable answers.)

The phonics lesson is the long *e* sound as in the word *he*. Other words from the story are: *the, eat, tree, tweet,* and *see*. Notice long *e* words can have an *e, ea,* or *ee* spelling.

Answers: 1. yellow 2. white 3. brown 4. black 5. blue

Who Took the Bird's Nest?, p. 15

Complete the following sentences by writing in the missing color word. See if you can spell them from memory.

1. The y_____ bird built a nest.

2. She asked the w_____ cow if she took the nest.

3. Br_____ Dog did not take it either.

4. Bl_____ Sheep gave wool to make the nest soft.

5. The little boy felt bl_____ because he took the nest.

THE MOUSE, THE CRICKET, AND THE BEE, p. 21

Preteach and review vocabulary: cricket, bee, plan, light, dark, sunshine, corn, buzz, chirp, and squeak.

Answer the following comprehension questions.

Literal

1. Where did the cricket want to build a house and why? The cricket wanted to build a house under the barn because it was dark there.

Literal

2. Where did the bee want to build a house and why? The bee wanted to build a house in a tall tree in the meadow because it was light there.

Vocabulary

3. What is a *meadow*? A meadow is a flat piece of land covered with grass.

Implied

4. Why is Bee happy that there are flowers in the meadow? Bee was happy because bees use flowers for food.

Literal

5. Where did the mouse want to build a house and why? The mouse wanted to build a house on the ground in the cornfield so she could play in the sunshine and eat corn.

Literal

6. What season was it? How do you know? It was spring because Mouse said that winter was over.

Implied

7. How do you know this story is not real? This story is not real because a mouse, cricket, and bee cannot talk to each other.

Creative

8. Where would you build a house if you could build one anywhere you wanted? Why? (Accept all answers.)

The phonics lesson is the long *i* sound found in the word *like*. Other long *i* words are: *I, find, hiding, light, high,* and the second vowel sound in *sunshine*. Long *i* words can have a final *e* and can have the *igh* spelling.

Answers: 1. I 2. J 3. A 4. C 5. B 6. G 7. E 8. F 9. D 10. H

THE MOUSE, THE CRICKET, AND THE BEE, P. 21

Light and dark are examples of words that are opposites. Match each word to its opposite by putting the chosen letter next to the number.

_____	1. happy	A.	big
_____	2. good	B.	cool
_____	3. little	C.	under
_____	4. over	D.	always
_____	5. warm	E.	ugly
_____	6. tall	F.	no
_____	7. pretty	G.	short
_____	8. yes	H.	work
_____	9. never	I.	sad
_____	10. play	J.	bad

BOBBIE'S YELLOW CHICKEN, p. 26

Preteach and review vocabulary: proud, summer, cried, farm, barn, and laughed.

Answer the following comprehension questions.

Literal

1. Who does Bobbie live with during the summer and where is it? Bobbie lives with his grandmother on her farm during the summer.

Implied

2. Where do you think Bobbie lives the other times of the year? Bobbie probably lives in the city because he was excited about being on the farm.

Literal

3. What does Grandmother give Bobbie? Grandmother gives Bobbie a little yellow chicken.

Implied

4. Why does Bobbie have to wait for his chicken to lay an egg for him? Bobbie has to wait for his chicken to lay an egg because the chicken is still a baby.

Implied

5. Why did Bobbie have trouble finding his little chicken when he went to his grandmother's farm the next summer? Bobbie did not know his chicken because she had grown up.

Literal

6. How did the big brown hen feel after she laid Bobbie an egg? The big brown hen felt proud.

Vocabulary

7. Tell about a time when you felt proud. (Accept any answers.)

Creative

8. What do you think Bobbie will do with all the eggs his chicken lays for him? (Accept any reasonable answers.)

The phonics lesson is a review of the long *a, e* and *i* sounds.

Answers: First D, Next B, Then A, Finally C

BOBBIE'S YELLOW CHICKEN, P. 26

When you sequence things, you put them in order of how they happened. Sequence the following statements next to the given words by cutting out the statements for the story and pasting them where they belong. Keep the letter that matches attached for checking purposes.

First_____

Next_____

Then_____

Finally_____

A. Bobbie went home until the next summer.

B. Bobbie gave the chicken food and water every day.

C. Bobbie came back and the chicken had grown up and was laying eggs for him.

D. Bobbie's grandmother gave him a little yellow chicken.

THE GO-TO-SLEEP STORY, P. 31

Preteach and review vocabulary: downy, green, doggie, cunning, keep, creep, leap, deep, peep, and asleep.

Answer the following comprehension questions.

Literal

1. Who was the first character to go check on Baby Ray? Little dog Penny was the first character to check on Baby Ray.

Literal

2. What was Baby Ray's mother telling him? Baby Ray's mother was telling him a go-to-sleep story.

Implied

3. How old do you think Baby Ray is? Why? Baby Ray is probably two or three years old because he is old enough to feed the animals but young enough to be called Baby Ray and take naps.

Implied

4. Where do you think Baby Ray lives? Baby Ray probably lives on a farm or in the country since he has a dog, kittens, bunnies, geese, and chicks.

Literal

5. What does Baby Ray give the kittens for their dinner? Baby Ray gives the kittens milk for their dinner.

Vocabulary

6. What might kittens do that is cunning? Kittens might learn how to open the bag of food or figure out how to push a door open. (Accept other reasonable answers.)

Literal

7. What does Baby Ray give the bunnies for dinner? Baby Ray gives the bunnies green leaves for dinner.

Implied

8. Where do the four geese live? The four geese live in the duck pond.

Vocabulary

9. The five little chicks were downy. Explain what downy means. Downy means that the chick's feathers were very soft and fluffy.

The phonics lesson is the long *o* sound found in the word *go*. Another word from this story is *so*. The long *e* sound with the *ee* spelling can be reviewed with the words *keep, creep, deep, peep,* and *asleep*.

Answers: one, two, three, four

Check drawings for the correct number of objects.

THE GO-TO-SLEEP STORY, P. 31

This story contains some number words. Write each number word and draw a picture that show that number of objects. Be sure to spell each word correctly.

1._____

2._____

3._____

4._____

A LULLABY, p. 37

Preteach and review the following vocabulary: flowers, closed, lullaby, lambs, stars, and moon.

There are no comprehension questions for this story.

Check out a tape of lullabies at your local library to rest or relax to.

The phonics lesson is the long *o* sound again. This selection has the words *oh* and *closed*.

THE ANT AND THE DOVE, P. 38

Preteach and review the following vocabulary: water, ant, once, tumbled, help, safe, and leaf.

Answer the following comprehension questions.

Literal

1. What was the ant's problem? The ant's problem was that she tumbled into the cold brook.

Implied

2. Why did the man keep very still while trying to catch the dove? The man kept very still while trying to catch the dove so the dove would not notice him.

Literal

3. How did the ant help the dove? The ant helped the dove by biting the man so he would jump. When he jumped, Dove saw him and flew away.

Implied

4. Why was the ant happy that the dove was safe? Ant was happy because Dove had helped her and now she had helped Dove.

Creative

5. Tell about a time when someone helped you and later you helped them. (Accept any reasonable answers.)

The phonics lesson is the *th* blend. This story contains these *th* blend words: *the, thank, then,* and *threw*.

Answer: Statement 4 is the main idea.

THE ANT AND THE DOVE, P. 38

The main idea of a story is the main thing the author wants to say. Below you will find four statements from the story. One statement is the main idea, and the other three are the details of the story. Circle the one statement that is the main idea of the story. Reread the story if needed.

1. An ant went to the brook.

2. The dove helped the ant.

3. Later the ant helped the dove.

4. The ant and the dove helped each other because they were friends.

THE PROUD LEAVES, P. 40

Preteach and review the following vocabulary: cool, shade, below, roots, new, and voice.

Answer the following comprehension questions.

Literal

1. Tell two reasons why the leaves were proud. The leaves were proud because they were beautiful, made a cool shade for boys and girls, and because birds sing to them and build their nests all around. (Accept any two.)

Implied

2. How does the wind sing through the leaves? The wind sings by blowing the leaves, which makes a rustling sound.

Literal

3. Who spoke to the leaves in a soft, little voice? The roots spoke to the leaves in a soft, little voice.

Implied

4. What do the leaves learn from the roots? The leaves learn that the roots keep the tree alive.

Creative

5. What lesson, or moral, could you learn from this story? You might learn that even though something works quietly and is not very beautiful, it is still very important. (Accept any reasonable answers.)

The phonics lesson is the long *e* sound spelled with *ea,* as in the word *leaves*.

Answers: Accept any nouns and verbs given. Three more words from the story could be from these: *leaves, roots, shade, fly,* and *spring*.

THE PROUD LEAVES, P. 40

Nouns are words that name a person, place, or thing. *Cat, house, playground,* **and** *paper* **are nouns. Verbs are words that tell about an action.** *Run, eat, sneeze,* **and** *yell* **are verbs. Find five more nouns and verbs from the story and list them here.**

NOUNS	VERBS

1. _____   1. _____

2. _____   2. _____

3. _____   3. _____

4. _____   4. _____

5. _____   5. _____

Some words can be used as a noun or a verb. *Swing* **is an example of one such word. The** *swing* **in the back yard is fun. This sentence shows** *swing* **as a noun. I** *swing* **with my legs out in front. This sentence shows** *swing* **as a verb. See if you can find three more words like this from the story.**

1. _____

2. _____

3. _____

THE DOG AND HIS SHADOW, p. 42

Preteach and review the following vocabulary: bone, mouth, shadow, and bridge.

Answer the following comprehension questions.

Literal

1. What did the big dog always do when he got a bone? The big dog always hid the bone.

Implied

2. Why would the big dog hide his bones? The big dog hid his bones because he didn't want any other dogs to have them.

Literal

3. What did the big dog think he saw when he looked into the water? The dig dog thought he saw another dog with a bone, but it was only his reflection in the water.

Implied

4. What is the moral of this fable? It doesn't pay to be greedy and not share.

Creative

5. Tell about a time that someone would not share and how it made you feel. (Accept any reasonable answers.)

The phonics lesson is a review with the long *o* sound. Words from this story are: *shadow, bone, go, so, own,* and *over*.

Answers: Accept any reasonable adjectives in the blanks. You may substitute *an* for *a* if needed.

THE DOG AND HIS SHADOW, P. 42

An adjective is a describing word. The *little* bug sat on the *red* flower. The words in *italics* are adjectives. In the following sentences, fill in the blank with an adjective.

1. If he saw a dog with a _____ bone, he would take it.

2. The big dog ran to the _____ brook.

3. The dog ran out on a _____ bridge.

4. The bone fell out of his _____ mouth.

5. The _____ dog could not get it.

THE KITE AND THE BUTTERFLY, P. 44

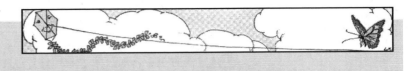

Preteach and review the following vocabulary: kite, clouds, string, and butterfly.

There are no comprehension questions for this story.

The phonics lessons is the long *i* sound spelled with *ie* and *y*. Words for this lesson are: *tied, fried, butterfly,* and *fly*.

Answers:
1. grandfather 2. sunshine 3. raindrop 4. playground 5. birthday
6. toothbrush 7. inside 8. airplane 9. sidewalk 10. football

THE KITE AND THE BUTTERFLY, P. 44

Compound words are when two words are joined as one. *Butterfly* is a compound word made from the words *butter* and *fly*. Cut the words from the bottom of the page and glue them next to a word that makes a compound word. Choose three to illustrate on the back of the page.

1. grand

2. sun

3. rain

4. play

5. birth

6. tooth

7. in

8. air

9. side

10. foot

| drop | ground | father | day | plane |

| brush | side | shine | walk | ball |

THE CAT AND THE FOX, p. 45

Preteach and review the following vocabulary: fox, woods, cross, foolish, tricks, safe, noise, and hunter.

Answer the following comprehension questions.

Literal

1. What were the cat and fox looking for in the woods? The cat and fox were looking for food. The cat wanted a fat mouse, and the fox wanted a fat rabbit.

Implied

2. Why was the fox cross? The fox was cross because he could not find a rabbit.

Vocabulary

3. What are two other words that mean about the same as cross? Mad and angry mean about the same as cross. (Accept any other reasonable answers.)

Implied

4. How did the cat feel about being unable to find a mouse? Cat felt patient when she couldn't find a mouse. When she wanted a mouse, she could wait.

Literal

5. Why did the fox think he could always get along? The fox thought he could always get along because he knew many tricks.

Literal

6. What one trick did the cat know? The one trick the cat knew was to jump when the dogs came.

Implied

7. Why did the fox want to teach the cat some of his tricks? The fox wanted to teach the cat some of his tricks because he thought his many tricks were better than the cat's one trick.

Literal

8. When the dogs came, what happened to the cat and the fox? When the dogs came, Cat jumped into a tree and was safe. Fox was caught by the dogs.

Implied

9. What is the moral of this story? The moral of the story is that sometimes knowing one thing well is better than knowing many things.

Creative

10. If you were the fox, how would you get away from the dogs? (Accept reasonable answers.)

The phonics lesson is the short *a* sound found in the word *cat*. *Fat, rabbit, had, at, can*, and *catch* are other words from the story with short *a* sounds.

Answers: Accept any reasonable sentences.

THE CAT AND THE FOX, p. 45

Adding *ed* to a word means it has already happened—it is in the past. Read the following sentences. Write your own sentences using the italicized words with an *ed* or *ing* added.

1. I *want* a present.

    _____

2. We *laugh* at funny jokes.

    _____

3. Can we *look* at your picture?

    _____

4. The horse can *jump* over the fence.

    _____

5. We will *play* a trick on our friends.

    _____

A WISH, P. 48

Preteach and review the following vocabulary: legs, short, slow, worms, and hawk.

Have the student answer the following comprehension questions.

Literal

1. What does May wish for? May wishes she had wings so she could fly.

Implied

2. Why does May dislike going up high hills? May dislikes going up high hills because it is tiring.

Implied

3. Who helps May realize that being a girl is best for her? Mother Bird helps May realize that it is best for her to be a girl.

Literal

4. What would May have to eat if she were a bird? May would have to eat worms.

Creative

5. If you could have one wish, what would it be? (Accept any answers.)

The phonics lesson is the short *i* sound as in the word *wish*. Other words include: *wings, hill, dinner, think, milk, little, wind, it,* and *is.*

Answers: May—I sleep in a bed. I eat bread and milk. Both—I have legs. I can walk. Bird—I can fly. I eat worms. I have wings. I sleep in a tree.

A WISH, P. 48

A Venn diagram is two or more circles that cross over one another. These diagrams are used to compare two or more things. Use the Venn diagram below and the given statements to compare May and the bird from the story. Put the statements that fit both May and the bird in the space where the circles cross. Cut out the sentences and glue them in the correct place.

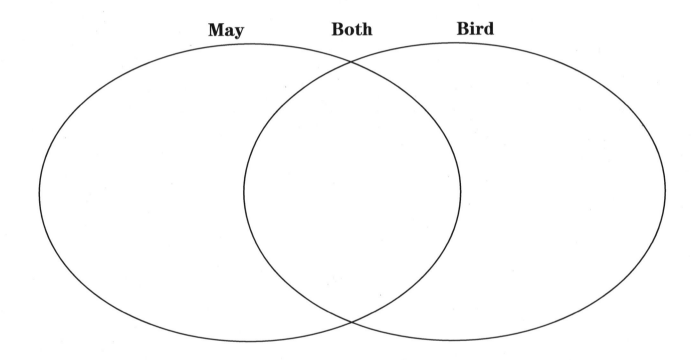

May   Both   Bird

I have legs.   I have wings.   I sleep in a tree.

I can fly.   I can walk.   I sleep in a bed.

I eat worms.   I eat bread and milk.

Molly and the Pail of Milk,

p. 50

Preteach and review the following vocabulary: pail, money, hens, hatched, buy, sell, and counted.

Have the student answer the following comprehension questions.

Literal

1. Who gave Molly the pail of milk? Molly's mother gave her the pail of milk.

Literal

2. What did Molly plan to do with the money she earned from selling the milk? Molly planned to buy eggs and hatch them.

Implied

3. How was Molly going to earn enough money to buy a farm? Molly was going to earn the money to buy a farm by selling the chickens that hatched. She would use the money from the chickens to buy many, many eggs so she would have many, many chickens to sell.

Literal

4. What keeps Molly from selling her pail of milk? When Molly jumps and sings, she drops her pail of milk.

Implied

5. Why was Molly jumping and singing? Molly was jumping and singing because she was excited about her idea of buying a farm.

Creative

6. How could a person your age earn money to buy something special? (Accept any reasonable answers.)

The phonics lesson is the short *e* sound found in the word *get*. Some other words that match this sound are *eggs, head, sell,* and *hens.*

Answers: 2, 5, 3, 1, 4

MOLLY AND THE PAIL OF MILK, P. 50

Read the sentences below. Number them 1–5 to show the sequence of the story.

_____ Molly planned to buy some eggs.

_____ Molly spilled the milk, and her plan was ruined.

_____ The eggs would hatch, and the chicks would grow up.

_____ Molly's mother gave her a pail of milk to sell.

_____ Molly would sell the chickens to get more money.

THE FINE PLAN p. 53

Preteach and review the following vocabulary: patter, feet, afraid, plan, bell, neck, joy, and wise.

Have your child answer the following comprehension questions.
Literal

1. What problem did the mice in this story have? The problem for the mice was that a big cat kept catching them.
Literal

2. What "fine plan" did the little mice have? The "fine plan" was that they should put a bell around the cat's neck so they could hear him coming.
Literal

3. What was the problem with the mice's "fine plan"? The problem with the little fine plan was no one wanted to be the one to hang the bell around the cat's neck.
Implied

4. What might the moral of this story be? The moral might be that when you think you have a great idea be sure to think it through to the end. (Accept other reasonable answers)
Creative

5. What advice do you have for the mice on how to keep from being caught by the cat? (Accept all reasonable answers.)

The phonics lesson is a review of the short *a, e,* and *i* sounds. Words we found with short *a* are: *plan, ran, cat, catch, cannot, shall, that, than,* and *fast.* Words with short *e* are: *bell, every, neck, yes,* and *then.* Words with short *i* sounds are: *big, lived, him, this, little, it,* and *will.*

Answers: 1. jumping 2. catch 3. eat 4. laughing 5. hanging 6. walk 7. know 8. hear 9. saying 10. squeaking

THE FINE PLAN, p. 53

Fill in the blank with the correct form of each word.

1. I am _____ on my trampoline.
   (jump, jumping)

2. The cat tried to _____ the mice.
   (catch, catching)

3. Are you going to _____ that candy
   bar? (eat, eating)

4. The boys and girls are _____ at
   the movie. (laugh, laughing)

5. Your coat is _____ on the door.
   (hang, hanging)

6. May we _____ to the store?
   (walk, walking)

7. I _____ how to ride a bike.
   (know, knowing)

8. Can you _____ the ice cream truck? (hear, hearing)

9. Listen to what your mother is _____. (say, saying)

10. My brother's mouse is _____ because he is hungry. (squeak, squeaking)

THE RACE, P. 56

Preteach and review the following vocabulary: hare, tortoise, river, race, warm, and hopped.

Answer the following comprehension questions.

Literal

1. Who are the main characters in this story? The main characters are Hare and Tortoise.

Literal

2. Where do Tortoise and Hare race? The tortoise and hare race to the river.

Literal

3. Why does Hare lose the race? Hare loses the race because he stops to eat and sleep.

Vocabulary

4. What other animal is very similar to a hare? A rabbit is an animal that is similar to a hare.

Implied

5. What time of year do you think it is? Why? It is probably summer because it is a very warm day.

Implied

6. What is the moral of the story? The moral is working at a steady pace is better than working fast, a little here and there.

The phonics lesson is to compare the short *o* and the long *o* sounds. Words with short *o* are: *on, stop, some, not, off, hop,* and *long.* Words with long *o* are: *slow, only, woke, so,* and *old.*

Answers: beginning—meadow, end—river

THE RACE, P. 56

The setting of a story is where it takes place. Sometimes a story has many settings. This story has one setting at the beginning and a different setting at the end of the story. Illustrate each of these settings below.

Setting at the beginning of the story

Setting at the end of the story

THE COCK AND THE FOX, p. 59

Preteach and review the following vocabulary: cock, friend, news, top, beasts, birds, flapped, called, and haste.

Have your child answer the following comprehension questions.

Literal

1. What was the cock doing on top of the barn? The cock was on top of the barn flapping his wings and crowing.

Literal

2. How did the fox try to trick the cock into coming down? The fox tried to trick the cock by telling him the beasts and birds are going to live together and not hurt each other any more.

Implied

3. How did the cock trick the fox? The cock tricked the fox by pretending to see dogs coming.

Vocabulary

4. Tell about a time you moved with great haste. (Accept reasonable answers.)

Creative

5. What do you think fox will do when he realizes he has been tricked? (Accept any reasonable answers.)

The phonics lesson is the short *o* sound. *Fox, cock, top, not, got, dog,* and *off* are short *o* words.

Answers: 1. do + not 2. will + not 3. can + not 4. did + not 5. could + not 6. would + not

THE COCK AND THE FOX, p. 59

Read the contractions below. Write the two words that make the contraction. For example, is + not = isn't.

1. _____ + _____ = don't

2. _____ + _____ = won't

3. _____ + _____ = can't

4. _____ + _____ = didn't

5. _____ + _____ = couldn't

6. _____ + _____ = wouldn't

THANKSGIVING IN THE HENHOUSE P. 62

Preteach and review the following vocabulary: Thanksgiving, henhouse, forget, snow, cracks, year, loud, basket, wheat, and evening.

Have your child answer the following comprehension questions.

Literal

1. What day is it in the story? It is Thanksgiving Day in the story.

Literal

2. What did Jack do to help the animals stay warm? Jack filled all the cracks in the henhouse to help keep the animals warm.

Implied

3. Why are Brown Hen, Gray Goose, and Little Chick unhappy? Brown Hen, Gray Goose, and Little Chick are unhappy because they are hungry and cold, and they think Jack has forgotten them.

Implied

4. Why do you think Jack forgot to feed the animals? Jack probably forgot to feed the animals because he was so excited about it being Thanksgiving Day.

Implied

5. Why did Red Cock suggest the animals sing a glad Thanksgiving song? Red Cock may have suggested the animals sing a song to cheer themselves up, or maybe Red Cock knew the noise would get Jack's attention.

Literal

6. Who tells Jack to take the animals some food? Jack's father reminds him to feed the animals.

Vocabulary

7. Name some things you do in the evening. (Accept any reasonable answers.)

Creative

8. What do you and your family do on Thanksgiving Day? (Accept any answers.)

The phonics lesson is on the short *u* sound as in the word *run*. Other words from the story include: *must, us, up, hungry,* and *cut.*

Answers: 1. C 2. A 3. E 4. G 5. F 6. D 7. B

THANKSGIVING IN THE HENHOUSE, p. 62

This story has many characters. Characters are people or animals in a story who do something. Match the character with the description.

1. Brown Hen   A. tried to cheer the other animals

2. Red Cock   B. gave the animals water

3. Big Turkey   C. didn't like to eat snow

4. Mother   D. gave the animals corn and wheat

5. Father   E. thought Brown Hen and Gray Goose were too cross

6. Jack   F. reminded Jack to feed the animals

7. Mary   G. thought the henhouse was noisy

THE CHRISTMAS FAIRY, p. 67

Preteach and review the following vocabulary: Christmas, fairy, cones, tired, rest, shook, prettiest, shine, and gold.

Have your child answer the following comprehension questions.

Implied

1. What month does this story take place? How do you know? This story takes place in December because it is two days before Christmas, and Christmas is always in December.

Literal

2. Why did the children go into the woods? The children went into the woods to find a Christmas tree.

Literal

3. Why were the children looking for a tree with many cones on it? The children were looking for a tree with cones because they had nothing else to put on their tree.

Implied

4. Why could the children not find their way home? The children could not find their way home because it was dark.

Literal

5. Who came right up to the children? A Christmas Fairy came to the children.

Literal

6. Why was the Christmas Fairy in the woods at Christmas time? The Christmas Fairy was in the woods at Christmas time to make the woods bright at night so good boys and girls can find the prettiest trees.

Implied

7. What was special about the beautiful tree that the Christmas Fairy helped the children find? The tree that the Christmas Fairy helped the children find was special because it had cones that were shining, and they would light the way home.

Vocabulary

8. Use shook in a sentence. (Accept any reasonable answers.)

Creative

9. How would you decorate a Christmas tree to make it beautiful? (Accept any answers.)

The phonics lesson includes the *br* and *tr* blends. Two examples from the story are *bright* and *tree*.

An extension to this story is to draw and decorate your special Christmas tree.

Answers: Problem: The children were trying to find a Christmas tree with lots of cones and got lost.

Solution: The Christmas Fairy found the children a tree that would light the way home.

THE CHRISTMAS FAIRY, p. 67

Most stories have problems that have to be solved. Write or illustrate the problem in this story. Then write or illustrate how the problem was solved.

Problem

Solution

BABY'S STOCKING, p. 71

Preteach and review the following vocabulary: stocking, corner, Santa, and goodies.

There are no comprehension questions for this story.

The phonics lesson is the *st* blend found in the word *stocking*.

Answers: yet, year, toe   (Accept any three pairs of words that rhyme.)

BABY'S STOCKING, P. 71

**Find the rhyming words from the story. Then think of three more pairs
of rhyming words.**

forget _____

here _____

go _____

_____ _____

_____ _____

_____ _____

THE BIG MAN AND THE LITTLE BIRDS, P. 72

Preteach and review the following vocabulary: tall, country, road, and Abraham Lincoln.

Have your child answer the following comprehension questions.

Literal

1. Where were the tall man and his friends riding their horses? The tall man and his friends were riding along a country road.

Implied

2. What time of the year do you think it was? Why? It was probably spring because birds usually have their babies in spring.

Literal

3. What did the tall man do with the baby birds? The tall man put the baby birds back in their nest.

Implied

4. What did the tall man mean when he said, "I could not have slept tonight if I had not helped her."? The tall man meant that he would have felt bad about not helping the bird, and he would have worried so much he would have trouble sleeping.

Creative

5. Tell two other things you know about Abraham Lincoln.

The phonics lesson is the *sl* blend found in the word *slept*.

THE BIG MAN AND THE LITTLE BIRDS, P. 72

Look up facts about Abraham Lincoln. Use an encyclopedia, the Internet, or books from the library for your research. Use your new knowledge to write a paragraph about him on this page.

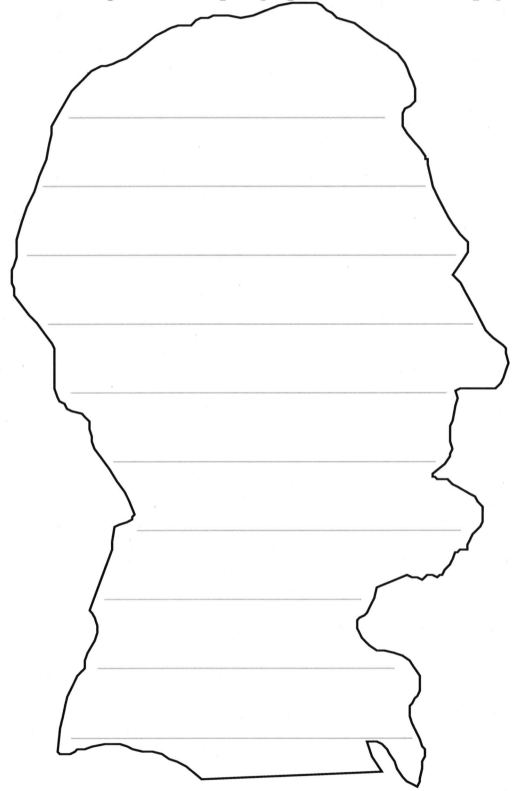

Our Flag, p. 74

Preteach and review the following vocabulary: flag, land, hue, hurrah, and stripes.

There are no comprehension questions for this story.

The phonics lesson is the *fl* blend found in the word *flag*.

Have your child draw or construct an American flag. One suggestion is to use torn paper in red, white, and blue. Your child can glue the pieces on a big piece of paper in the shape of a flag.

AMERICA, p. 75

Preteach and review the following vocabulary: liberty, pilgrim, pride, and freedom.

There are no comprehension questions for this story.

The phonics lesson includes the blends *fr* and *pr* found in the words *freedom* and *pride*.

AMERICA, p. 75

Memorize and recite this poem clearly. Use available resources to look up facts about Flag Day. Use the space provided to record three facts learned in complete sentences.

1. _____

   _____

   _____

2. _____

   _____

   _____

3. _____

   _____

   _____

THE PARADE ON WASHINGTON'S BIRTHDAY, P. 76

Preteach and review the following vocabulary: grandfather, grandmother, window, parade, street, and George Washington.

Have your child answer the following comprehension questions.

Literal

1. Where did Father get the old flag? Father got the old flag from Grandfather and Grandmother.

Literal

2. Why couldn't Father take Ned and Patty to the parade? Father could not take Ned and Patty to the parade because Grandmother was sick and he had to go see her.

Implied

3. Where was Grandmother when Mother and Father went to see her? How do you know? Grandmother was probably in the hospital. Mother and Father went to see her right away, she was probably very sick, and very sick people are usually in the hospital.

Implied

4. Do you think Ned and Patty lived in the city or country? Why? Ned and Patty lived in the city because the parade came down the street where they lived.

Creative

5. Describe the last parade that you saw. (Accept any reasonable answers.)

The phonics lesson is the blend *gr* from the words *grandmother, grandfather,* and *great.*

THE PARADE ON WASHINGTON'S BIRTDAY, P. 76

Use available resources to look up facts about George Washington. Write a short paragraph about him in the space provided.

THE LITTLE RED HEN, P. 79

Preteach and review the following vocabulary: grain, wheat, turkey, ripe, reap, thresh, mill, flour, and bread.

Have your child answer the following comprehension questions.

Literal

1. Who did Little Red Hen ask to help her with the wheat? Little Red Hen asked the dog, cat, pig, and turkey to help her.

Vocabulary

2. What does the story mean by "Little Red Hen reaped the wheat"? It means that Little Red Hen was cutting and gathering the wheat.

Literal

3. Why did Little Red Hen take the wheat to the mill? Little Red Hen took the wheat to the mill to have it ground into flour.

Implied

4. The main character in a story is the person or animal the story is mainly about. Who is the main character in this story? How do you know? Little Red Hen is the main character in this story because the story is mainly about her and the adventure she has with the bread.

Implied

5. What time of year does this story take place? This story probably takes place in the fall because that is when most crops are harvested.

Creative

6. Little Red Hen and her chicks ate the loaf of bread. Should Little Red Hen have shared her loaf of bread with the other animals? Tell why you think she should or should not share. (Accept any reasonable answers.)

The phonics lesson is the blend *wh* from the word *wheat*.

Answers: Main Character—The main character is Little Red Hen. Setting—The story takes place at a farm because of all the farm animals around. Problem—Little Red Hen cannot get anyone to help her make the bread. Solution—Little Red Hen let her chicks help her eat the loaf of bread.

THE LITTLE RED HEN, P. 79

Illustrate the main character, setting, problem, and solution from the story. Write a sentence to go with your illustrations.

Main Character

Setting

Problem

Solution

THE LOST EGG, p. 83

Preteach and review the following vocabulary: six, seven, eight, nine, ten, shells, garden, fast, and ground.

Have your child answer the following comprehension questions.

Literal

1. What did Brownie have in the barn? Brownie had a soft nest in the barn.

Implied

2. Why did Brownie sit on her nest so long? Brownie sat on her nest for a long time because she was keeping her eggs warm so they would hatch.

Literal

3. What was Brownie's problem? Brownie's problem was that she had ten eggs but only nine chicks.

Implied

4. Why did Brownie go see Bobbie and his mother? Brownie probably went to see Bobbie and his mother because she thought they could help her.

Literal

5. Where did Bobbie find the missing chick? Bobbie found the missing chick in the nest, still in the egg.

Vocabulary

6. What is another word for *hark*? Another word for *hark* is *listen*.

Literal

7. What did Bobbie do with the chick after it came out of its shell? Bobbie gave the chick to Brownie to put under her wing after it came out of its shell.

Implied

8. How did all the other little chickens show they were happy? The other little chickens showed they were happy by running and flapping their wings.

Creative

9. Do you think Bobbie should have picked up the egg that was left in the nest? Tell why or why not. (Accept any reasonable answers.)

The phonics lesson is the *sh* blend from the words *she* and *shell.*

THE LOST EGG, P. 83

**Write each number word in the blank. Be sure to spell them correctly.
Then draw pictures to match each number.**

6 _____

7 _____

8 _____

9 _____

10 _____

The Goats in the Turnip Field, p. 86

Preteach and review the following vocabulary: goats, turnip, field, wolf, and grass.

Have your child answer the following comprehension questions.

Literal

1. Where did the boy take his goats every morning? Every morning the boy took his goats to a hill so they could eat the green grass.

Implied

2. Why would the goats not leave the turnip field? The goats would not leave the turnip field because the turnips really tasted good to them, and they did not get to eat turnips every day.

Vocabulary

3. Draw a picture of a turnip. (Drawing should include green leaves and a white root.)

Literal

4. What animals tried to help the boy? The rabbit, fox, wolf, and bee tried to help the boy.

Literal

5. How did the boy and other animals react when the bee offered to get the goats out of the turnip field? The boy and other animals laughed at the bee when he offered to help.

Implied

6. Why do you think the boy and animals laughed at the bee? The boy and animals laughed at the bee because all of them were much bigger than the bee, and they had not been able to get the goats out of the field.

Implied

7. Why did the goats run out of the field and all the way home when the bee said "Buzz-z-z"? The goats ran all the way home when the bee said buzz because they were afraid the bee would sting them.

Creative

8. What lesson do you think the boy learned that day? The lesson is that no matter how small something is, it is important and can be helpful. (Accept other reasonable answers.)

The phonics lesson is the *cr* blend found in the words *cry, cries,* and *crying.* You may want to take an opportunity to talk about the difference between the three words given and have your child make up sentences to distinguish between them.

Answers: human, animal/number of legs/hop, walk, fly/pets, not a pet/characters with or without tails (Accept any other reasonable classifications.)

THE GOATS IN THE TURNIP FIELD, P. 86

Think of three different ways to classify the characters from the story. (Example: insect—bee).

Group 1   _____

Group 2   _____

Group 3   _____

THE KIND CRANES, P. 90

Preteach and review the following vocabulary: hungry, sea, fish, cranes, strong, beaks, and claws.

Have your child answer the following comprehension questions.

Literal

1. Why did the six little birds want to cross the sea? The six little birds wanted to cross the sea so they could get fat worms.

Implied

2. Why did the little birds decide not to go with the fish? The little birds decided not to go with the fish because he would take them down into the sea, and the little birds knew they would drown.

Literal

3. What two reasons did the sheep give the birds for being unable to take them across the sea? The sheep could not take the birds across the sea because he never swam, and he could not fly.

Literal

4. Why did the first crane tell the little birds to ask the last crane to take them across the sea? The first crane told the little birds to ask the last crane because the first crane's back was full.

Implied

5. Why did the first crane tell the little birds to ask the last crane instead of the second or third? The first crane told the little birds to ask the last crane because the second and third cranes' backs were full, too.

Literal

6. How did the little birds hang on to the crane? The little birds hung on to the crane with their beaks and claws.

Vocabulary

7. What is another word for sea? Another word for sea is ocean.

Creative

8. Why do you think the cranes helped the little birds across the sea? (Accept any reasonable answers.)

The phonics lesson is a review of the blends *cr* and *sh*. You may even want your child to find words that end with the *sh* blend.

Answers: First, they asked the fish. Next, they asked the sheep. Then, they asked the crane. Finally, the crane took them across.

THE KIND CRANES, P. 90

Fill in the blanks to retell the story. Use sequencing words to help you
tell it in order. You have been given the first and last sentences.

Six little birds wanted to cross the ocean to get fat worms.

First, _____

Next, _____

Then, _____

Finally, _____

The birds found all the worms they could eat.

THE NORTH WIND, P. 94

Preteach and review the following vocabulary: robins, reason, hark, lark, and wren.

There are no comprehension questions for this story.

The phonics lesson is the *ch* blend from the word *chick-a-dee*.

Answers: south, hurry, cold

THE NORTH WIND, P. 94

Fill in the blanks with facts from the story.

1. **Robins, meadow larks, and wrens fly** _____
    when it turns cold.

2. **If the meadow lark must make haste, then he must**

    _____.

3. **Chick-a-dee is not afraid of the** _____.

WHAT DOES LITTLE BIRDIE SAY?, P. 96

Preteach and review the following vocabulary: rise, limbs, longer, and stronger.

Have your child answer the following comprehension questions.

Literal

1. What does Little Birdie want to do? Little Birdie wants to fly away.

Implied

2. What does the author mean by "peep of the day"? The author uses "peep of the day" to mean early in the morning.

Literal

3. What does Mother Bird suggest when Birdie wants to fly away? Mother Bird suggests that she rest a little longer so her wings will be stronger.

Implied

4. How are Little Baby and Little Birdie similar? Little Baby and Little Birdie are similar because they both want to fly away.

Implied

5. How would a baby "rise and fly away"? The author is using this phrase to mean the baby wants to grow up and be on its own.

The phonics lesson is the *str* blend from the word *stronger*.

Answers: long, longer, longest; strong, stronger, strongest; old, older, oldest; little, littler, littlest

WHAT DOES LITTLE BIRDIE SAY?, P. 96

When you want to compare two things, you use *-er* at the end of the
describing word. If you want to compare more than two things,
you use *-est* at the end of the describing word. Add *-er* and *-est* to
the following words to make new describing words. Choose one
set of words to illustrate.

long _____ _____

strong _____ _____

old _____ _____

little _____ _____

The Hen and the Squirrel, p. 98

Preteach and review the following vocabulary: squirrel, acorns, cloth, head, baker, and forest.

Have your child answer the following comprehension questions.

Literal

1. What do the hen and squirrel do at the beginning of the story? At the beginning of the story, Hen and Squirrel decide to get acorns to eat from a tall oak tree.

Implied

2. In what season does this story take place? How do you know? This story takes place in the fall because that is when oak trees have lots of acorns.

Literal

3. Who is the first person the hen asks for help? The first person the hen asks for help is an old woman.

Implied

4. Why did the hen want to tie up her head with a soft cloth? The hen wanted to tie up her head with a soft cloth to stop the bleeding and to keep the cut clean.

Literal

5. What did the dog want before he would give the hen two hairs? The dog wanted some bread before he would give the hen two hairs.

Implied

6. Why did the baker want wood before he would give the hen bread? The baker probably wanted the wood to use in his ovens so he could bake more food.

Vocabulary

7. Tell three things you might find in a forest. (Accept any reasonable answers.)

Literal

8. What did the brook want in exchange for the water? The brook wanted nothing from the hen.

Creative

9. After the hen gives everyone what they asked for, she ties up her head. What do you think she will do next? The hen might lay down and rest after all her troubles. (Accept any other reasonable answers.)

The phonics lesson is the *sq* blend from the word *squirrel*.

Answers: 1. B 2. D 3. A 4. C

THE HEN AND THE SQUIRREL, P. 98

Usually when something happens, something else caused it to happen. This is called cause and effect. *The egg broke because it fell off the table.* "It fell off the table" is the cause, and "the egg broke" is the effect. Match the following cause and effect statements from the story.

1. ___ Hen and Squirrel ran to the tree   A.   because Squirrel threw down big acorns.

2. ___ Hen couldn't reach the acorns   B.   because the tree was full of acorns.

3. ___ Hen's head was cut   C.   because her head was cut.

4. ___ He needed a soft cloth   E.   because she couldn't fly so high.

THE PINE TREE AND ITS NEEDLES, p. 103

Preteach and review the following vocabulary: pine, needles, bag, glass, and wish.

Have your child answer the following comprehension questions.

Literal

1. What kind of leaves did the pine tree wish for first? The pine tree wished for gold leaves first.

Implied

2. Why did the man take all of the pine tree's gold leaves? The man took the pine tree's gold leaves because he thought they were beautiful and worth a lot of money.

Literal

3. What kind of leaves did the pine tree wish for next? The pine tree wished for glass leaves next.

Implied

4. How did the wind break the glass leaves? The wind broke the glass leaves by blowing the leaves against each other and against the branches of the tree.

Literal

5. What kind of tree had big green leaves like Little Pine Tree wanted? The oak tree had big green leaves like Little Pine Tree wanted.

Literal

6. At the end of the story, what kind of leaves did Little Pine Tree decide were best for him? At the end of the story, Little Pine Tree decided little pine needles were best for him.

Creative

7. Why do you think the fairy kept giving the pine tree his wishes? (Accept any reasonable answers.)

The phonics lesson is the *bl* blend found in the words *blue* and *black*.

Answers: 1. G 2. F 3. I 4. H 5. D 6. B 7. C 8. E 9. A 10. J

THE PINE TREE AND ITS NEEDLES, p. 103

You add *-ed* to most words to show past tense. However, there are some words that don't follow this pattern. See if you can match the word with its past tense.

1. _____ come   A. blew

2. _____ have   B. saw

3. _____ take   C. ate

4. _____ shine   D. broke

5. _____ break   E. went

6. _____ see   F. had

7. _____ eat   G. came

8. _____ go   H. shone

9. _____ blow   I. took

10. _____ say   J. said

How Gosling Learned to Swim, _{P. 107}

Preteach and review the following vocabulary: gosling, pond, quack, duckling, colt, bark, and calf.

Have your child answer the following comprehension questions.

Literal

1. Why did Little Gosling go into the pond? Little Gosling went into the pond to learn to swim.

Implied

2. Why did the chicken peep while Gosling swam? The chicken peeped while Gosling was swimming because chicks are supposed to peep. He was practicing his peeping, so he would become good at it.

Literal

3. Name three other animals besides the gosling who practiced something. The chicken, duckling, rabbit , colt, dove, dog, and calf all practiced something. (Accept any three.)

Vocabulary

4. Use leap in a sentence. (Accept any reasonable answers.)

Creative

5. What is something you practice? (Accept any reasonable answers.)

The phonics lesson is the blend *ck* found in the middle of the words *chicken* and *duckling* and at the end of the words *quack* and *chick*.

HOW GOSLING LEARNED TO SWIM, P. 107

Cut out each animal picture and glue into groups. Write a sentence under each group telling why the animals belong to that group.

I Don't Care, p. 110

Preteach and review the following vocabulary: gate, open, world, cart, and another.

Have your child answer the following comprehension questions.

Literal

1. Who lives in the meadow? A horse and a brown colt live in the meadow.

Literal

2. Why does the colt want to leave the meadow? The colt wants to leave the meadow because he thinks he will have more fun down the road.

Implied

3. Why did the old white horse tell the colt to stay in the meadow? The old white horse told the colt to stay in the meadow because he knew it was safer there.

Literal

4. What did the old white horse think about the colt running down the road? The old white horse thought the colt should return to the meadow because he was too little to see the world.

Literal

5. Where did the colt run after talking to Old White Horse and the mule? The colt ran to town after talking to Old White Horse and the mule.

Vocabulary

6. What is a town? A town is a small city.

Literal

7. How did the colt feel about the town? The colt felt scared by the town.

Implied

8. Why did the colt run into the glass? The colt ran into the glass because he thought he saw another colt and he was going to ask him the way to the meadow.

Creative

9. Do you think Little Colt will listen to the other animals when they give him advice next time? Why or why not? (Accept any reasonable answers.)

The phonics lesson is the *pl* blend from the words *place* and *play*.

For an extension to this story, your child can write his or her own version of Eric Carle's "Brown Bear, Brown Bear, What Do You See?"

I Don't Care, p. 110

Homophones are words that sound the same but are spelled differently and have different meanings. Pick a homophone from each pair and write a sentence using each word correctly.

here	know	right	won	not	seen	too	son	road	by
hear	no	write	one	knot	scene	two	sun	rode	bye

1. _____

2. _____

3. _____

4. _____

5. _____

6. _____

7. _____

8. _____

9. _____

10. _____

THE CAMEL AND THE PIG, p. 114

Preteach and review the following vocabulary: camel, short, hump, snort, and fruit.

Have your child answer the following comprehension questions.

Literal

1. What was the camel proud of in the story? The camel was proud that he was tall.

Literal

2. What was the pig proud of in the story? The pig was proud that he was short.

Literal

3. What did the animals say they would give up if they were not right? The camel said he would give up his hump, and the pig said he would give up his snout.

Implied

4. Is this story fact or fiction? How do you know? This story is fiction because animals cannot talk the way the animals talked in this story.

Implied

5. How did being tall help the camel get the fruit from the first garden? Being tall helped the camel because he was able to reach his neck over and get the fruit.

Literal

6. How was the pig able to get into the second garden? The pig was able to get into the second garden by going through the gate.

Implied

7. Why did the camel keep his hump and the pig keep his snout? The camel kept his hump and the pig kept his snout because they were both right.

Creative

8. Would you rather be tall or short? Tell why. (Accept any reasonable answers.)

The phonics lesson is the *sn* blend from the word *snout*.

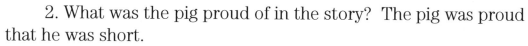

Answers: Camel—tall, hump, long neck; Pig—short, snout; Both—proud, animals got fruit (Accept any other correct comparisons.)

THE CAMEL AND THE PIG, p. 114

Using the Venn diagram, compare and contrast the camel and the pig from the story.

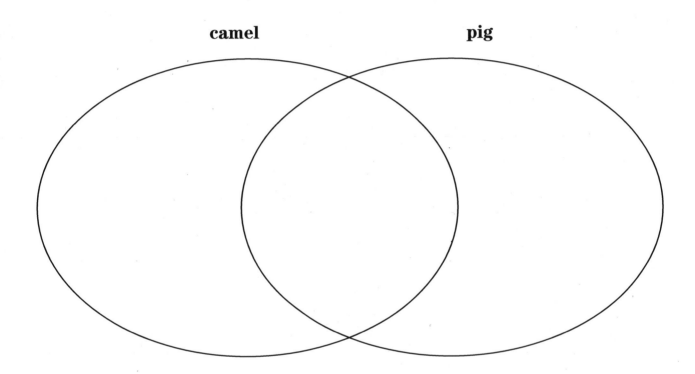

THE LITTLE ROOSTER, p. 118

Preteach and review the following vocabulary: rooster, crow, hairbrush, comb, and weed.

Have your child answer the following comprehension questions.

Literal

1. What did the little rooster like to do? The little rooster liked to crow.

Implied

2. How did the man feel about the rooster's crowing? The rooster's crowing made the man angry because it woke him up.

Literal

3. What did the man do the first time Rooster made him angry? The man threw a hairbrush at the rooster the first time he made the man angry.

Vocabulary

4. Explain a comb on a rooster. A rooster has a comb on top of his head.

Literal

5. What did the man do with the rooster at the end of the story? At the end of the story, the man gave the rooster away.

Implied

6. Why did the weeds grow up and fill the man's garden? Since the rooster was gone, the man slept more instead of working in his garden, and the weeds grew up and filled the garden.

Creative

7. Do you think the man handled his anger correctly? Tell why or why not? (Accept any reasonable answers.)

The phonics lesson is the *oo* sound from the words *rooster* and *doodle*.

Answers: 1. I'll 2. we'll 3. they'll 4. don't 5. didn't 6. aren't 7. I've 8. could've 9. she's 10. we're

THE LITTLE ROOSTER, P. 118

Read the following words. Write the contraction for the words. Example:
is not **will be changed to** ***isn't.*** **Practice saying each contraction clearly.**

1. I will _____

2. we will _____

3. they will _____

4. do not _____

5. did not _____

6. are not _____

7. I have _____

8. could have _____

9. she is _____

10. we are _____

NORTH WIND AT PLAY, p. 122

Preteach and review the following vocabulary: work, lily, lilies, puff, buds, and rough.

Have your child answer the following comprehension questions.

Literal

1. What did North Wind want to do one summer day? North Wind wanted to play one summer day.

Literal

2. What three characters did North Wind ask to play? North Wind asked the apple tree, the corn, and a lily to play with him.

Implied

3. How was the apple tree helping the apples to grow? The apple tree was helping the apples to grow by giving the apples food and water through its branches.

Literal

4. What did North Wind do when the corn said it could not play? North Wind blew the corn down when it said it could not play.

Vocabulary

5. What is a lily? A lily is a plant with funnel shaped flowers.

Implied

6. Why could the lily not look up again after North Wind blew her down? The lily could not look up again after North Wind blew her down because her stalk was probably broken.

Implied

7. How does this story explain why a northern wind blows mostly in winter? This story explains northern winds in winter by telling that North Wind has to wait until the apples, corn, and lilies are gone before it can go out and play.

Creative

8. What do you think the apple tree, corn, and lily did after North Wind left? (Accept reasonable answers.)

The phonics lesson is a review of the blends *pl* and *bl* as in *plan* and *blue*.

As an extension to this legend, have your child tell about the weather where you live. Then he or she can make up a legend that explains why the weather is that way.

Answers: 1 ? 2 . 3 ! 4 . 5 ?
1. flies 2. buggies 3. cries 4. babies 5. ladies

NORTH WIND AT PLAY, P. 122

Write a period, exclamation mark, or question mark after each sentence
Example: What a noise the carts make _!_

1. What time is it _____

2. We got lost in the woods _____

3. What big paws the bear has _____

4. They tried to catch him _____

5. Why are you here _____

In the story, *lily* (one flower) has to be changed to *lilies* (more than one flower). Notice the *y* was dropped and *ies* was added to mean more than one. This happens because there is a consonant before the *y*. Change the following words by dropping the *y* and adding *ies*.

1. fly _____

2. buggy _____

3. cry _____

4. baby _____

5. lady _____

Three Billy Goats Gruff,

p. 126

Preteach and review the following vocabulary: Billy, Gruff, troll, tripping, gobble, second, and bigger.

Have your child answer the following comprehension questions.

Literal

1. Why did the Three Billy Goats Gruff go up the hill every day? The Three Billy Goats Gruff went up the hill every day to eat the grass and grow fat.

Literal

2. Why was everyone afraid of the troll? Everyone was afraid of the troll because he was so big and cross.

Implied

3. Why did Little Billy Goat Gruff tell the troll that his brother was bigger than he? Little Billy Goat Gruff told the troll that his brother was bigger so the troll would want to eat his brother instead of him.

Literal

4. What did Second Billy Goat Gruff tell the troll when the troll said he was going to gobble him up? Second Billy Goat Gruff told the troll to wait for Big Billy Goat Gruff.

Implied

5. Was Big Billy Goat Gruff scared of the troll? Tell how you know. Big Billy Goat Gruff was not scared of the troll. I know because Big Billy Goat Gruff told the troll to "come along" when the troll threatened to gobble him up.

Implied

6. What did the troll mean when he told the Billy Goats Gruff "be off with you"? When the troll told the goats "be off with you," he meant that they should leave or be on their way.

Vocabulary

7. Write a sentence about something you would like to gobble. (Accept any answer.)

Creative

8. What do you think the troll did after he ran away from Big Billy Goat Gruff? (Accept any reasonable answers.)

The phonics lesson is a review of the *gr* and *tr* blends found in the words *gruff* and *troll*.

For an extension to this story, make finger puppets out of available materials and retell the story.

Answers: first, 2nd, third, fourth, 5th, sixth, 7th, eighth, 9th, tenth

THREE BILLY GOATS GRUFF, p. 126

This story has the ordinal words *first*, *second*, and *third*. Ordinal words show position. Fill in the missing ordinal word or abbreviation.

1st   _____

_____   second

3rd   _____

4th   _____

_____   fifth

6th   _____

_____   seventh

8th   _____

_____   ninth

10th   _____

THE LITTLE PLANT, p. 131

Preteach and review the following vocabulary: heart, seed, buried, raindrops, and rose.

There are no comprehension questions for this poem.

The phonics lesson is the long *i* sound spelled with *igh,* as in the words *light* and *bright*.

Your child can memorize and recite this poem. A tip to help with memorization is to see if the poem fits a well-known song. The tune to "Mary Had a Little Lamb" fits with this poem.

THE SWING, p. 132

Preteach and review the following vocabulary: air, pleasantest, child, cattle, and roof.

There are no comprehension questions for this poem.

The phonics lesson is the *sw* blend from the word *swing*.

Answers: 1. capitalized 2. rhymes 3. Accept any two rhyming words from the poem. 4. paragraphs or sentences 5. three

THE SWING, P. 132

Fill in the blanks and learn some rules of poetry.

1. In a poem, the first letter of the first word in every line is

   _____

2. Poetry often _____, but it does not always.

3. Two words that rhyme in "The Swing" are _____

   and _____.

4. Poetry has verses; stories have _____.

5. "The Swing" has _____ verses.

THE SLEEPING APPLE, p. 134

Preteach and review the following vocabulary: kiss, golden, and cheeks.

Have your child answer the following comprehension questions.

Literal

1. Where was the little apple? The little apple was hanging high in an apple tree.

Implied

2. What was the little girl's problem? The little girl's problem was that she wanted the apple to wake up, but it kept sleeping.

Literal

3. How long did the sun try to wake the apple? The sun tried to wake the apple until it turned golden yellow.

Implied

4. Why do you think the robin flew to the apple tree? The robin probably flew to the apple tree because she was looking for food for her babies.

Literal

5. Who did the girl hear coming through the trees? The girl heard the wind coming through the trees.

Implied

6. How could the wind wake someone at night? The wind could wake someone by blowing limbs up against a house or making noises as it blew through the cracks of a house.

Creative

7. What do you think the girl will do now that the apple is awake? (Accept reasonable answers.)

The phonics lesson is the *ing* ending from the words *sleeping* and *morning*.

Answers: 1. grew 2. slept 3. came 4. flew 5. sang 6. cheered 7. thanked 8. tried 9. fell 10. shook

THE SLEEPING APPLE, P. 134

Read the following sentences. Write the past tense form of the verb on the line. Some verbs are regular and need an *ed* added. The other verbs are irregular and have a different form.

1. The plant _____ very quickly. (grow)

2. The baby _____ all night. (sleep)

3. We _____ home after dark. (come)

4. Yesterday, a bird _____ into our house. (fly)

5. We _____ in church on Sunday. (sing)

6. My friend _____ me up. (cheer)

7. I _____ Grandmother for my gift. (thank)

8. Our team lost even though we _____ hard. (try)

9. The book _____ off the shelf. (fall)

10. The building _____ during the earthquake. (shake)

SWEET PORRIDGE, P. 138

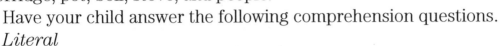

Preteach and review the following vocabulary: supper, fire, sweet, porridge, pot, boil, stove, and people.

Have your child answer the following comprehension questions.

Literal

1. Why did the little girl and her mother sometimes have no supper? The little girl and her mother sometimes had no supper because they were very poor.

Implied

2. If the girl had no food to cook, why was she looking for wood for a fire? The little girl was looking for wood for the fire because she and her mother needed to keep warm.

Literal

3. Who did the little girl see in the woods? The little girl saw an old woman with a little black pot in the woods.

Implied

4. What was special about the little black pot? The little black pot was special because it would cook the girl all the sweet porridge she wanted without the girl putting anything in the pot.

Literal

5. What did the mother forget when she used the pot? When the mother used the pot she forgot how to make it stop.

Vocabulary

6. Use the word *flowed* in a sentence. (Accept reasonable answers.)

Creative

7. How do you think the other people felt about the streets being full of sweet porridge? Why? (Accept reasonable answers.)

The phonics lesson is the *dge* blend found at the end of *porridge* and *bridge*.

Answers: 1. "Oh, I wish I had some sweet porridge!" she said. 2. She said, "Little girl, why are you so sad?" 3. "I am hungry," said the little girl. 4. Then the little girl said, "Little pot, stop!" 5. "Now," they said, "we are happy we shall not be hungry any more."

SWEET PORRIDGE, p. 138

When someone is speaking in a story you will see quotation marks. They mark the beginning and ending of what a person has said. Read these sentences from the story. See if you can put the quotation marks in the correct place.

1. Oh, I wish I had some sweet porridge! she said.

2. She said, Little girl, why are you so sad?

3. I am hungry, said the little girl.

4. Then the little girl said, Little pot, stop!

5. Now, they said, we are happy we shall not be hungry anymore.

JOHNNY-CAKE, P. 144

Preteach and review the following vocabulary: Johnny-cake, spade, hoe, door, rolled, and woof.

Have your child answer the following comprehension questions.

Literal

1. What were the little old man, little old woman, and little boy going to do with the Johnny-cake? The little old man, little old woman, and little boy were going to eat the Johnny-cake for supper.

Vocabulary

2. For what would you use a spade and hoe? You use a spade and hoe to remove weeds, to break up the ground, or to dig.

Implied

3. Why did the boy forget about Johnny-cake? The boy forgot about Johnny-cake because no one was inside to remind him. He may have gotten busy doing other things and forgot.

Literal

4. Who was the first animal Johnny-cake met? The first animal Johnny-cake met was the hen.

Literal

5. Why do the hen and cow chase Johnny-cake? The hen and cow chase Johnny-cake because they want to eat him.

Implied

6. How does the pig trick Johnny-cake? The pig tricks Johnny-cake because he is so sleepy, Johnny-cake keeps coming closer trying to make the pig listen. Johnny-cake gets closer and closer until the pig eats him up.

Implied

7. What is the setting of this story? How do you know? The setting of this story is on a farm because there is a garden and farm animals.

Creative

8. If you were a character in the story, how would you catch Johnny-cake? (Accept reasonable answers.)

The phonics lesson is the *sp* blend from the word *spade*.

Answers: 1. woman, man, and boy 2. hen 3. cow 4. pig

JOHNNY-CAKE, p. 144

Cut and glue the pictures to show the sequence of characters who wanted eat Johnny-cake.

1

2

3

4

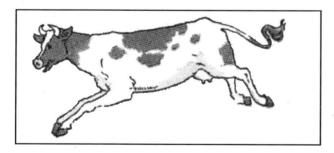

MARY AND THE LARK, p. 150

Preteach and review the following vocabulary: Mary, Tiny, south, east, and west.

Have your child answer the following comprehension questions.

Literal

1. How many baby birds are in the lark's nest? There are three baby birds in the lark's nest.

Implied

2. What does the mother bird mean when she says all the birdies are very good? When the mother bird says all the birdies are very good, she means they are all well behaved and do what they are supposed to do.

Literal

3. Why does Mary want to take Tiny Beak home? Mary wants to take Tiny Beak home to play.

Implied

4. Why does the lark tell Mary she could take Tiny Beak if Mary brought her Baby Alice? The lark told Mary she could take Tiny Beak if Mary brought her Baby Alice because she wanted Mary to realize that Tiny Beak needs to stay in his home, just like Baby Alice needs to stay in her home.

Creative

5. Where do you think Mary will go after her visit with the birds? (Accept reasonable answers.)

The phonics lesson is the blend *thr* from the words *three* and *threw*.

Answers: words that need capital letters—Mary, Their, Tiny Beak, Light Wing, Bright Eyes, Mary, Their, Alice, and Ned

MARY AND THE LARK, p. 150

A sentence always begins with a capital letter. Names also begin with capitals. People's names and names of specific places are called proper nouns. Circle the words that need capital letters in the following paragraph. Hint: You will find twelve words that need to be capitalized.

mary saw some birdies in a nest. their names were tiny beak, light wing, and bright eyes. mary told the birdies about the children in her house, too. their names were alice and ned.

THE HEN WHO WENT TO HIGH DOVER, p. 153

Preteach and review the following vocabulary: dream, High Dover, den, feather, and chimney.

Have your child answer the following comprehension questions.

Literal

1. What did Henny Penny dream? Henny Penny dreamed that she would find a nest of golden eggs if she went to High Dover.

Literal

2. What characters does Henny Penny meet on her way to find the golden eggs? Henny Penny meets Cocky Locky, Ducky Lucky, Gandy Pandy, and Foxy Woxy on her way to find the golden eggs.

Implied

3. Do you think the first four characters Henny Penny meets believed that she would find the golden eggs? Why or why not? Yes, the animals believed Henny Penny would find golden eggs because they went with her.

Implied

4. Why do you think the animals wanted to go with Henny Penny? The animals wanted to go with Henny Penny because they wanted some of the golden eggs.

Vocabulary

5. What is a gander? A gander is a male goose.

Literal

6. What did the fox tell Henny Penny when she told him about her dream and finding golden eggs? The fox told Henny Penny she was foolish when she told the fox about her dream.

Literal

7. What happened to the duck and gander while they were sleeping in the fox's den? The fox ate the duck and gander while they were sleeping in his den.

Literal

8. How did Henny Penny save herself and Cocky Locky? Henny Penny saved herself and Cocky Locky by tricking the fox. She told the fox that she saw geese flying by. While he ran out to see, Henny Penny and Cocky Locky escaped through the chimney.

Creative

9. Do you think the characters used good judgment when they

went to sleep in the fox's den? Why or why not? (Accept reasonable answers.)

The phonics lesson is the *dr* blend from the word *dreamed*.

Answers: Accept reasonable responses and make sure they are capitalized.

THE HEN WHO WENT TO HIGH DOVER, P. 153

Proper nouns often name people or specific places. Proper nouns are capitalized. Look at the nouns below and think of a proper noun to go with them. Don't forget to capitalize in the correct places. Example: school—Wayside Elementary

1. state _____

2. city _____

3. store _____

4. church _____

5. hospital _____

6. street _____

7. country _____

8. doctor _____

9. celebrity _____

10. friend _____

HANSEL'S COAT, p. 161

Preteach and review the following vocabulary: Hansel, curly, thorns, straight, sew, spin, threads, scissors, and crab.

Have your child answer the following comprehension questions.

Implied

1. Why is Hansel cold? Hansel is cold because he has no coat to wear.

Literal

2. How does the sheep help Hansel? The sheep helps Hansel by giving him wool for his coat.

Literal

3. How was the curly wool made straight and soft? The curly wool was made straight and soft after Hansel pulled it through the thorn bush.

Literal

4. How did Spider help Hansel? Spider helped Hansel by spinning the wool into threads and then making it into cloth.

Implied

5. What does Crab mean when he says his claws are like scissors? When Crab says his claws are like scissors he means they are sharp and can cut material.

Implied

6. Why does Bird sew her nest together every spring? Bird sews her nest together every spring so she can lay eggs and raise her babies there.

Creative

7. Why do you think Hansel's mother could not get him a coat until winter? (Accept reasonable answers.)

The phonics lesson is the blend *cl* from the word *cloth*.

Answers: Accept reasonable adjectives to match the nouns.

HANSEL'S COAT, P. 161

Adjectives are words that describe nouns. Write two adjectives that describe the following nouns. Example: cold, spring morning.

1. _____ coat.

2. _____ winter.

3. _____ sheep.

4. _____ wool.

5. _____ thorns.

THE LAMBKIN, p. 164

Preteach and review the following vocabulary: Lambkin, Granny, jackal, tender, I'll, we'll, tiger, promised, skin, corn-bin, and didn't.

Have your child answer the following comprehension questions.

Literal

1. Why was Lambkin going to Granny's? Lambkin was going to get good things to eat and get fatter and fatter.

Vocabulary

2. Use the word *wee* in a sentence. (Accept reasonable answers.)

Literal

3. Who wants to eat Lambkin? The jackal, tiger, wolf, and dog want to eat Lambkin.

Implied

4. How many weeks did Lambkin stay in the corn-bin? How do you know? Lambkin stayed in the corn-bin one week because the story says he stayed there seven days and seven days make a week.

Implied

5. Why did Granny tell Lambkin he must go home? Granny told Lambkin he had to go home because he had been gone a week and his family was probably worried.

Literal

6. How did Lambkin get home? Lambkin got home by hiding in a drumkin and rolling home.

Implied

7. Which character did not fall for Lambkin's trick? Why? The jackal did not fall for Lambkin's trick because he was wise and recognized Lambkin's voice.

Creative

8. If you were Lambkin, how would you have gotten home from Granny's? (Accept reasonable answers.)

Answers: jackal, tiger, wolf, and dog. A wolf is a villain in the Three Little Pigs and Little Red Riding Hood. Accept any other stories where a wolf is the villain.

THE LAMBKIN, P. 164

Many stories have at least one villain. A villain is a character who does mean things. Name the four villains in this story.

1. _____

2. _____

3. _____

4. _____

Can you think of two other stories where a wolf is the villain? Name them.

1. _____

2. _____

SNOW-FLAKES, p. 172

Preteach and review the following vocabulary: sky and swiftly.

There are no comprehension questions for this story.

The phonics lesson is the *er* ending as in the word *feather*.

Answers: Accept reasonable, interesting words.

SNOW-FLAKES, p. 172

When people write, they use interesting words to tell their stories. Replace the underlined word with an interesting word to spice up the sentence. Example: Our dog is <u>big</u>. gigantic.

1. The birds flew <u>fast</u>. _____

2. The baby is <u>cute</u>. _____

3. The <u>pretty</u> woman is dancing. _____

4. The pie tastes <u>good</u>. _____

5. My brother was <u>bad</u> at the show. _____

THE CLOUDS, p. 173

Preteach and review the following vocabulary: stand and away.

Have your child memorize and recite this poem. "Rock-a-bye Baby's" tune can be used to help with the memorization process.

The phonics lesson is a review of the *wh* blend from the word *white*.

WORD LIST

The following list contains the words of *Book One* that were not taught in the *Primer*. Many of these words have been developed phonetically in earlier lessons, and are therefore not new to the child when read on the pages indicated. Such words are printed in italic type.

9 Gustava
spring
sun

10 more
here

11 glad
over

12 food
but
threw

13 this
yet

14 just

15 tweet-tweet
yellow
shall
if

16 such
beautiful
sorry

17 hairs
never

18 soft
prettiest
ever

19 think
hung
head
hid

20 felt
very
again
as

21 cricket
bee
plan

22 place
chirp
light
try

23 sunshine
tall
buzz

24 field
fun
together

25 high
best
hiding
squeak

26 summer
many
always
great

27 every
lay
an
grew

28 please
when

29 waiting
cried
own

30 off
laughed
proud

31 Penny
first
baby
story
doggie
given

32 our
cunning
kitty-cats
creep

33 bunnies
green
leap

34 geese
duck-pond
deep

35 five
chicks

36 downy
crying

37 lullaby
closed
lambs
stars
moon
fall

38 ant
leaf
got
blew
sometime

39 catch
kept
near
bit
safe

40 cool
shade
swing
through

41 voice
below
roots
die
new
should

42 bone
across
hide

43 bridge
thought
fell
seen
shadow

44 kite
clouds
butterfly
tied
string

45 *met*
fox
fat
mice
getting

46 foolish
right
tricks
ha
better
than

47 noise
hunter
running
barking
only

48 legs
short
slow
walk
long

49 sure
worms
tree-top
shakes
hawk

50 Molly
pail
sell
money
buy
hatched

51 build

52 began
poor
counted
until

53 patter
caught
afraid

54 fine
hang
bell
neck
ting-a-ling
joy

55 wise
old
wiser
way

56 hare
tortoise
river
swim
hop
race

57 nearly
rest
before

58 slept
hopped
beats

59 flapped
called
reach

60 friend
beasts
hurt
each
talk
knew

61 stayed
well
haste
won't

62 Thanks-
giving
indeed
hungry

63 *outside*
sad
year

64 turkey
song
cut-cut-ca-
da-cut
loud

65 *wheat*

66 children
evening

67 nothing
cones

68 tired
care
shook

69 *bright*
fairy
asked

70 gold
wonderful

71 stocking
darling
write
corner
Santa
goodies
toe

72 country
men

73 Abraham Lincoln

74 flags
hue

75 stripes

76 window
parade
George
Washington
birthday

77 last

78 street
told

79 grain
plant
grow
ripe

80 reap
thresh

81 flour
bake
loaf

83 Brownie
why
ten
breaking
nine

84 six
seven
eight

85 *hark*

86 goats
grass
turnip

87 because

88 wolf

90 sea
wide
fish
swam

91 cranes
strong
beaks

For more information visit us at: http://www.lostclassicsbooks.com